Shivers

D0833067

YOUR MOMMA'S
A WEREWOLF

M. D. Spenser

Paradise
Press, Inc.

Plantation, Florida

For Mom —
not a werewolf, but always an inspiration

ISBN 1-57657-095-9

EXCLUSIVE DISTRIBUTION BY PARADISE PRESS, INC.

Cover Design by George Paturzo
Cover Illustration by Eddie Roseboom

Printed in the U.S.A.

30622

Chapter One

My name is Ignatius J. Rockwell. My friends call me Iggy.

Well, they don't *always* call me Iggy. Sometimes they call me "Ignatius J." Because they know I can't stand it.

I prefer Iggy. That's what my mom calls me. She named me after two famous historical figures: Ignatius Loyola, the Catholic saint who founded an order of priests called the Jesuits, and Iggy Pop, the rock star from Detroit.

We live in Detroit, too. My mom used to know Iggy Pop, back when he sang in a band called the Stooges. She also went to an all-girls' high school run by the Jesuits. Hence, my unusual name.

I like it.

My mom always says it's better to be unusual than boring. She should know. She's sort of unusual herself. For a mom, anyway. At least compared to all the moms I've ever met.

A long, long time ago, my mom used to play drums in a punk rock band. I think it was in 1977. The band was called We Hate You.

"But we didn't *really* hate people," my mom insists whenever I ask her about it. "We just *pretended* we did. To shock the audience."

Still, back then, she sure looked mean. The band put out two record albums — not CDs or tapes, but old-fashioned vinyl records. My mom's picture is on the back cover of both.

On the first record, her hair color is listed as "shocking magenta," which turns out to be a sort of reddish-purple. On the second record, her head is completely shaved. On both records, she's gritting her teeth, practically snarling. She looks like someone you wouldn't want to bump into late at night in a dark alley.

These days, my mom teaches tenth grade English at Southlake High School. She has a very sensible hairstyle — neat bangs, cut short in the back — and it's light brown, her natural color.

She still wears a black leather jacket. But instead of ripped-up blue jeans and T-shirts that say "I'm a Mess," her closet is filled with pretty skirts and blouses.

And she smiles all — well, *most* of the time. On the days I bring home my report card, she usually doesn't smile.

I'll admit it. I'm not the best student in the world. Not that I'm *stupid* or anything. I'm just not interested in most of the stuff they teach at Mansfield Elementary, where I'll be in the fifth grade this fall.

I'd rather be reading an "Aqua-Man" comic or playing kick ball or watching "The Tick" than working on some boring homework assignment.

That's the downside of having a mom who is also a teacher. Sometimes she acts like I should be doing a lot better in school, just *because* she's a teacher.

But there's also an upside. Every summer, my mom gets three months off, just like me. And every summer, for as long as I can remember, we've taken a vacation together, usually for a whole month.

This summer, we decided to go Up North. In Detroit, "Up North" means the Northern part of Michigan.

In case you're a little rusty on your geography, Michigan is shaped like a giant mitten. (I probably wouldn't know if I didn't live here.) Detroit is toward the bottom of the mitten, close to the opening where you'd stick in your hand. Up North is the top part, where your fingers would eventually end up.

For this summer's vacation, my mom rented a cabin near Lake Huron for an entire month. She also said that I could invite one friend along.

I decided to invite my friend John. Except we all call John by his nickname: Mole.

Mole can be pretty unusual. But like I said, I've learned to appreciate unusual people.

Still, I definitely wasn't prepared for the news Mole brought just before we left for the cabin.

It crossed the line from unusual to . . . creepy.

Chapter Two

Like a real mole, Mole is near-sighted and lives underground.

Well, *practically* underground. He spends most of his time in his parents' basement, reading old history books or watching documentaries about World War II on the History Channel.

Mole loves history. You could say he's obsessed. And you wouldn't be exaggerating.

Some people are surprised that Mole and I are such good friends. On the surface, we seem to be opposites in every way.

Mole is tall, I'm kind of short. Mole is extremely pale, I have a ruddier complexion. Mole is shy and clumsy, I'm outgoing and fairly athletic. Mole is an excellent student. And I'm, well, not as motivated, like I've said.

But we get along great. Mole can be really

funny.

For one thing, he thinks he's royalty. "I'm a fifth cousin, twice-removed, of the Earl of Lothian," he insists to anyone who'll listen. And when the laughter starts, he gets all huffy and adds: "You won't be laughing so hard when I reclaim my ancestral throne."

Sometimes, if he's really mad, he'll throw in a final shot: "You peasant!"

To Mole, there's no worse insult than calling someone a peasant.

Anyway, about a week before we were supposed to leave for the cabin, Mole rode his bike over to my house. He had a dusty history book tucked under his arm. A thick one. And his always pale face looked very serious.

Uh-oh, I thought as I opened the door. I sense a history lecture coming.

Mole loved history so much, he was known to get carried away when he talked about it. Sometimes, he seemed to think that *everybody* was as interested in, say, the Prusso-Danish War as he was.

"Hey, Mole," I said with a grin. "Nice of you to stop by. Let me take that book for you. Then we can play some Ninten- . . . "

"Forget it, Iggy," Mole interrupted. He saw right through my ploy. "This is serious. I have to show you something."

I sighed. The last "serious" thing Mole showed me was "proof" that a Polish scholar invented the modern alphabet. It took about two hours for him to explain.

"All right," I agreed warily. "Step into my office."

We made our way down the hall to my messy room. I cleared some clothes off the bed and plopped down. "Just remember, I have to eat dinner in about four hours, so you'd better make this quick. What's up?"

Mole sneered from behind his thick glasses.

"*This* is what's up," he almost shouted, flipping open his book on the bed.

"Calm down, Mole," I said. "I'm only two feet away. I can hear you."

"Just look," Mole ordered, pointing at the page he'd opened. "When I heard about where we were going, I decided to do some research at the library."

Then he looked at me and added, "You know, that place where they have these things called

7

books, where people who read go." Mole can be very sarcastic sometimes.

"Ha-ha," I fake-laughed. Then my eyes drifted to the page. I noticed the heading, in bold, black script: Fort Deckerville.

"Hey!" I exclaimed. "That's where we're going next week. That's where the cabin is."

"Wow, you're smarter than you look," Mole snapped. "Read on."

I glowered at Mole, then turned back to the book.

The paragraph under the heading began this way:

The town of Fort Deckerville was named after a British fort established in 1761. About twenty years later, the soldiers stationed at the fort suddenly stopped communicating with other forts in the vicinity. A squadron was sent to Fort Deckerville to investigate.

When the squadron arrived, they found the fort deserted. There was no sign of a struggle. There were no bodies. The soldiers had simply disappeared.

What happened remains a mystery. Some believe Indians captured the soldiers. Others contend that rival French settlers may have attacked.

But many people are still convinced that there is only one explanation: the supernatural. The British squadron was so terrified by the empty fort that they burned it to the ground.

I stared up at Mole. He was practically shaking with excitement.

"The supernatural?" I asked. "Do they mean that some kind of ghost made those soldiers disappear?"

"Maybe," Mole stammered. "It could've been anything. An Indian curse. A spirit from the forest. *Vampires.*"

"Vampires?" I cried. "Do they even *have* vampires in Michigan?"

"Well, they could, I guess," Mole snapped. "I don't know. The point is, whatever made those soldiers disappear . . . "

He paused, then continued: "Whatever made those soldiers disappear *wasn't human.*"

Chapter Three

"We're here!" my mom called out from the front seat of the minivan.

Mole and I had fallen asleep in the back. It was a long drive from Detroit to Fort Deckerville — about seven hours — and we'd woken up early to get a good start.

After much discussion, we had decided not to tell my mom about the mystery of the fort.

"What if she freaks out and cancels the trip?" I argued. "I mean, I don't think she believes in ghosts or that kind of stuff. But you never know how grown-ups are going to react. We'd better not jinx it."

"I just hope we haven't *already* jinxed it," Mole gulped.

Did I mention what a coward Mole could be?

I was even more excited about seeing Fort Deckerville now that we knew the place's weird and spooky history. It was the kind of excitement that's mixed with fear — like riding a roller-coaster or staying up late to watch a scary movie on cable.

I rubbed my eyes and peered out the window as the van rolled to a stop.

We were parked on a gravel driveway, surrounded by a thick forest. A medium-sized wooden cabin stood in the middle of a clearing. The cabin wasn't fancy, but it looked fairly solid.

We piled out of the van. I squinted in the sunlight. It was around dinner time. My stomach growled.

"Hey, Mom," I asked. "What's that little building over there?"

I pointed to a tiny wooden shack about the size of a closet. Not a very big closet, either. It stood a little ways from the cabin, closer to the edge of the forest.

"Um," my mom stuttered, biting her bright-red lip. I knew something was up. My mom was an English teacher. She didn't usually say "um."

"*That* building?" Mole asked, craning his neck forward like a turtle to get a better view. "Isn't that an . . . outhouse?"

"Now, guys," my mom began. "Let me explain."

"An outhouse?" I cried. "You mean this place doesn't have a real bathroom! No running water?"

"It has running water. And there's a bathroom, with a sink and a tub," my mom corrected. "But when the owner added those modern amenities, he decided to keep the outhouse. I think it's cute. And I didn't tell you about it because I knew you'd make a fuss."

I started to protest, but my mom cut me off.

"The key to the cabin is supposed to be hidden under that flower pot over there on the porch. Why don't we check it out first. Then you can complain all you want."

The inside of the cabin *was* pretty cool, I had to admit. It had a master bedroom for my mom and an upstairs loft where Mole and I would sleep.

Most of the space was taken up by a single, giant room — part kitchen, part dining room, part living room. It had an old-fashioned metal stove that burned wood. The floors were mostly wooden, with a few fuzzy rugs. Paintings of ducks and deer hung on the walls. A huge picture window looked out into the forest.

I was just starting to get used to the place

12

when I heard Mole, in an unusually timid voice, say, "No TV?"

My jaw dropped open.

He was right: There *was* no TV!

I dashed into the master bedroom and saw a bed, a dresser, a nightstand . . . but no TV.

I ran back into the living room.

"Mom?!" I cried. "What were you thinking!"

My mom grinned. She seemed to be enjoying our discoveries. "Well, I was thinking that it might do you both some good to spend a month without television, without talking on the phone . . . "

"No *phone*!" I cried.

"Nope," she said with a smile. "They have pay phones in town. And if your parents need to call us, John, they have the number of the rental agency."

"Well, there appears to be electricity, at least," Mole added hopefully, pointing at the light bulbs on the ceiling.

"Unless my mom decided to disconnect the power," I groused.

My mom laughed.

"No, we won't have to stock up on candles. There's electricity. But look, guys, you've got books and you've got each other. I brought a radio. And who needs TV when you've got *this*?"

She pointed at the picture window.

Outside, birds fluttered in the trees. The sun streamed down through the leaves. All of a sudden, a brown shape darted through the underbrush.

"Hey!" I cried. "Was that a deer!"

"Yeah, I think so," Mole called, running to the window. "Cool! I've never seen a deer before. I mean, other than at the petting zoo. But that doesn't count."

"Somehow, I don't think you'll be bored," my mom said.

"I guess I can survive a month without TV," I admitted. "How about you, Mole? Can you survive without the History Channel?"

I expected Mole to be upset with the idea of no History Channel for a month.

But not *this* upset: He responded with a blood-curdling scream!

Chapter Four

My mom and I dashed over to Mole. He was still standing in front of the picture window.

"John!" my mom cried. "What is it?"

Mole was even paler than usual and trembling all over. He pointed out at the forest.

"Di-didn't y-you see it?" he stuttered.

"No," I said. "We weren't even looking over here."

My mom put her hand on Mole's shoulder.

"What did you see, John?" she asked in her calmest voice.

Mole took a deep breath.

"Well, I was trying to see where that deer went," he said. "And then I caught a glimpse of it. Way back over there."

Mole pointed to a spot deep in the woods.

"It was standing perfectly still," he continued.

15

"I was about to call you guys to come over and look. And then, all of a sudden . . . " Mole's voice trailed off.

"What happened?" my mom and I asked at the same time.

"Something grabbed it," Mole stammered. "These hands . . . well, they didn't look like hands. They looked like *paws*. They came reaching out of the brush and grabbed the deer."

"I don't know," I said, trying not to sound too skeptical. "Aren't deer usually pretty fast?"

"That's the thing," Mole responded excitedly. "This, this . . . *whatever* it was just snatched the deer up before it even had a chance to move."

"So you're saying these arms you saw picked up an entire deer?" my mom asked.

"Like it was a Chihuahua," Mole insisted. "Like it was stuffed with feathers."

"Hmm," my mom mused, pulling thoughtfully on one of her silver hoop earrings. "The thing is, John, deer are usually quite heavy."

"*I* know that," Mole sniffed. "When Drofdarb the Obese killed a deer back in 1402, he had to drag it seven miles in the snow. Now history tells us . . . "

"But, Mo- . . . er, *John*," my mom interrupted. "Don't you think that maybe, just maybe, your glasses were a little steamed up and your imagination just ran a little wild?"

"No, Mrs. Rockwell, really, I know what I saw," Mole protested.

"Well, I'm sure you *think* you know what you saw," my mom began, "but couldn't those hands have been leaves? Couldn't the deer have been some branches?"

"I know what I saw," Mole repeated.

My mom frowned. "Have you guys been reading those horrible legends about the old fort?" she asked.

"How did you know about that?" I cried.

"The man who rented me this cabin sent down some brochures about Fort Deckerville," she said. "I didn't say anything about those old rumors because I figured you two would have overactive imaginations."

"But it wasn't my imagination, Mrs. Rockwell," Mole began.

"All right," my mom commanded, using her firmest teacher voice. "No more talk about monsters in the forest. Whatever happened at that fort happened two hundred years ago. We're here to have a good time. So let's finish unpacking and have some dinner. We'll all feel better after that."

As we headed back out to the van, I grabbed Mole by the sleeve and whispered, "Tomorrow, we look for the old fort."

Chapter Five

"So, what do you guys want to do today?" my mom asked after breakfast the next morning.

I glanced over at Mole, then said, "John and I were thinking of taking a hike in the woods."

Mole swallowed hard and began to fidget nervously with his glasses. I gave him a sharp kick under the table.

"Sounds good," my mom said. "Oh, Mr. Vincent, the owner of the cabin, stopped by this morning, while you were still asleep." She smiled. "I mentioned John's close encounter yesterday."

Mole perked up. "So what'd he say, Mrs. Rockwell? Has he heard of anything strange in these parts?"

"Welllll," my mom said, still smiling, "not exactly. He *does* think he knows what you saw, though."

She rose from the table and walked into the

living room area. Reaching behind the couch, she whisked out . . . a deer!

It was life-sized and perfectly real-looking, with antlers and all. Only it wasn't moving. I leaned over and rapped it with my knuckles. It was made of plastic!

"Does this look familiar, John?" my mom laughed. "Mr. Vincent said you probably saw *him* back there. He was cleaning up after the last people who rented this place. They were bow and arrow hunters. They use these fake deer for target practice."

Mole turned beet red.

"Well, from far away, they look pretty real," he began.

"Oh, don't be embarrassed, John," my mom said. "They *do* look real. I just don't want you guys to be worrying about some monster in the woods that doesn't exist. Enjoy yourselves. Have a good time. I think I'll do some target shooting myself. Then when it gets hot this afternoon, we can all go for a swim."

My mom doesn't hunt, but she likes guns. She keeps them locked up in a safe at home. I'm not allowed to go near them. But since our cabin was in such a secluded area, she decided to bring along her shotgun for some practice.

The night before, Mole and I had compared the map in his old book with a current map of the area. It looked like the old fort used to be somewhere in the forest nearby.

But it was hard to pinpoint anything exact from the maps. And we weren't even sure if any traces of the fort had survived the fire.

"But we have to at least *try* to find the fort," I'd insisted.

"I don't see why," Mole complained.

"Because it'll be an adventure," I cried. "Don't you ever want to have an adventure?"

"I prefer reading about other people's adventures," Mole said, before turning out the light. "It's safer."

We started our hike behind the cabin, where a trail wound deep into the forest.

It was a sunny morning. But the farther we went along the trail, the darker it became. Soon, the trees got so thick, only narrow shafts of sunlight poked through the branches.

"I think we'd better turn back, Iggy," Mole whimpered.

"I thought moles loved the dark," I shot back.

He squinted harshly at me, but kept walking.

Eventually, we came to a fork in the path. "This looks like a good place to take a break," Mole wheezed, and sat down on a rotten stump. Mole had read a lot of books, but he wasn't in the best shape in the world.

I leaned up against a tree on the opposite side of the path and pulled a sheet of paper out of the back pocket of my cut-offs. The night before, I'd jotted down some notes about the location of the fort.

After consulting the paper, I announced, "According to the maps, if we keep going in this direction, we should eventually hit the old fort."

"*If* there's anything left," Mole said.

"There have to be some clues lying around," I insisted.

"Whatever you say, Sherlo- . . . " Mole began.

Then his head bobbed forward and his jaw dropped wide open. He looked like an old-fashioned wooden puppet.

"What's the matter, Mole?" I asked, and started to make a joke about the goofy look on his face.

Then I heard the growling.
Coming from behind me.
Right behind me.
"Iggy," Mole finally screamed. "Look out!"

Chapter Six

I whirled around so fast that I tripped and stumbled into the middle of the path.

Lying on my back, propped up on my elbows, I caught my first glimpse of what had scared Mole so horribly.

It was a wolf.

But nothing like a cute cartoon wolf. Or a tame zoo wolf. Or even a big, bad fairy-tale wolf.

This was the biggest, meanest wolf I'd ever seen. Not that I'd *seen* lots of wolves running around suburban Detroit. But it was bigger than any wolf I could've imagined — as huge and muscular and fierce-looking as a tiger.

He crouched on all fours, just behind where I'd been standing. Leaves and twigs stuck to his gray fur.

Our eyes met. His were yellow. Gleaming.

24

Evil.

"Iggy." I heard Mole's voice, whispering from behind me. "Iggy. Don't move. Stay as still as possible. He'll only attack if he feels threatened."

I kept my eyes locked on the wolf.

Barely moving my lips, I muttered, slowly, through gritted teeth, "Are . . . you . . . sure?"

"No," Mole whispered. "This strategy might apply only to bears. But it seems to be working."

Mole was right. The wolf hadn't made any threatening moves since my fall. He seemed to be sizing me up.

I gulped, and tried not to move. Even though every muscle in my body screamed: *RUN, YOU DORK! YOU'RE IN A STARING MATCH WITH A WOLF!*

A mosquito landed on my nose.

No, I thought. This can't be happening!

Beads of sweat rolled down my forehead. I tried not to breathe. The mosquito started to crawl around, looking for the perfect place to feast.

Have you ever let a mosquito crawl around on your face? I didn't think so. But take my word for it — it tickles. A lot!

The wolf seemed to sense that I was getting

tense. He stared at me even harder. I stared back. But I was concentrating on my nose.

I'd go crazy if I couldn't scratch it soon!

The mosquito crawled down onto my upper lip. I clamped my mouth shut. No way I'm eating you, bug, I thought.

The wolf continued to stare at me.

The mosquito crawled up my left nostril.

NO! I thought, panicking. Get out of there!

I could feel the mosquito crawling around inside my nose. It tickled like crazy. Beads of sweat poured down my face. I started trembling all over.

As silently as possible, I tried to blow air through my nostril and dislodge my unwelcome guest.

Apparently, he wasn't ready to check out.

For a second, I couldn't feel anything.

Did it fly away without my noticing, I wondered hopefully. Then I panicked. Maybe he crawled up into my skull, onto my brain!

Then, just as quickly, my feeling of panic ended. It was replaced by a different feeling: pain!

The mosquito bit.

I howled and slapped my nose.
Mole screamed.
I looked back up.
The wolf pounced.

Chapter Seven

I couldn't see much.

Just a flash of gray fur. A glimmer of white fangs. And the yellow eyes disappearing in a blur.

There was no time to run. I barely had time to sit up. The wolf's two front paws hit me squarely in the chest.

I grunted and crashed back to the dirt, flat on my back.

Up close, the wolf's head was even bigger than it had looked. And he was *very* close. Directly above me.

He opened his mouth and growled, and I got a good look at his pink tongue, and his razor-sharp teeth. A blast of hot, stinking animal breath hit me in the face. I tried not to breathe.

A stream of slobber poured from the wolf's mouth and splashed me in the eyes. Everything got blurry. I couldn't move. I was pinned down fast by the wolf's paws.

He hovered over me, and growled again.

I'm dead, I thought.

Then I heard another scream. But it wasn't Mole's voice. It was my mom's! Where had she come from? Was I hallucinating? Maybe I was in shock!

I tried to look around, but I couldn't move. The wolf opened his mouth wide. He was getting ready to bite.

I heard a loud thump.

Then the wolf growled again. But this time, it was different. This time, it sounded like a yelp of pain.

"Get off my son, you creep!" a voice said. It was definitely my mom. Shouting. Right next to me.

I heard another thump. Suddenly, a huge weight lifted off my chest. The wolf had jumped off.

I rolled over and rubbed my eyes.

"Iggy, run, honey, run!" my mom was shouting.

I looked up and saw her standing a few feet away.

The wolf was about to pounce on top of her! The wolf was about to clamp its jaws around her throat!

Chapter Eight

"Mom!" I cried.

I couldn't tell what was happening. A blur of gray fur and black T-shirt and white fang and pink skin rolled around in the path in front of me.

"Iggy! Get out of the way!" Mole yelled. His voice came from behind me.

I whirled around and saw him standing in the path. He was holding my mom's shotgun.

"Move!" he shouted.

I realized I was standing between him and my mom and the wolf. I jumped off the path and almost fell down again.

As I turned around, I called out, "Don't hit my mom!"

But Mole was squeezing the trigger.

Have you ever fired a shotgun? I didn't think so. I haven't either. But believe me, they have quite a kick.

Just ask Mole.

When he fired the gun, the blast knocked him backwards. The noise, like a hundred cars backfiring at once, blotted out every other sound. My ears were filled with a dull ringing.

At first, I couldn't tell where the shot had landed. But I did see the wolf jump off my mom pretty quickly.

He stared at me for a split-second before bounding off into the woods, back where he came from. That was when I noticed the black singe marks on his tail.

Mole had grazed the wolf's behind!

I heard a moan from where Mole was lying. But I dashed in the opposite direction. Toward my mom.

She was lying on her back. Her eyes closed. Not moving.

"Oh, no!" I cried. "Sh-she's *d-dead*!"

<u>Chapter Nine</u>

I bolted over to my mom's body and fell to my knees beside her.

"No!" I shouted, choking back tears. "It can't be!"

I couldn't see any blood. But she wasn't moving. At all.

"Nooo!" I called out again. "She died saving me!"

Without any warning, my mom's eyes blinked open.

"Please, honey, don't yell," she murmured in a hoarse voice. "You know I can't handle loud noises the way I used to."

"Mom!" I cried, not caring much about her sensitive ears. "You're not dead!"

I threw my arms around her and squeezed her in a big bear hug.

"Easy, Iggy," she said with a laugh. "I will be

soon if you keep manhandling me." She leaned back and tousled my hair. "Are *you* all right?"

"I'm fine," I responded. "Just a little bruised. And scared."

"And Mole — er, *John*?" my mom asked. "How about you?"

Mole had picked himself up from the path and walked over to where we were sitting. He handed my mom her shotgun.

"I'm OK, Mrs. Rockwell," he said, then pointed at the side of her neck. "You're bleeding a little bit, though. Maybe we should get you to a doctor."

Sure enough, a trickle of blood ran down just below her right ear.

"Oh, it's just a nick," she insisted, dabbing at the bite with a handkerchief. "There's a first aid kit at the cabin. Let's walk back and bandage ourselves up."

As we made our way back along the trail, I explained to my mom how we had run into the wolf.

"Well, I was getting ready to do some target shooting when I heard John scream," my mom said. "I ran over here with my gun. But I didn't want to take the chance of hitting you, so I couldn't shoot at the wolf."

"She really clubbed it hard," Mole said. He sounded impressed.

"I used a thick branch. Then I wedged it into his mouth when he tried to bite me," my mom continued. "That's the only thing that kept him from tearing out my throat."

I shivered at the thought. But my mom smiled and looked at Mole.

"That, and this sharpshooter walking next to me," she said, patting him on the shoulder. "Thank you, John. You saved my life."

Mole blushed. He got embarrassed very easily.

"Oh, it was nothing, Mrs. Rockwell," he began.

"How'd you get to be such a good shot?" my mom asked. "You shouldn't be handling guns at your age."

"I've got a BB gun," Mole explained. "My dad lets me shoot cans in the backyard. I got pretty good, I guess."

Back at the cabin, my mom put a bandage on her neck. The bite wasn't deep, but we could make out faint teeth marks. She also disinfected a scrape on my knee. We spent the rest of the day sitting around and relaxing, recovering from our adventure. We went to bed early that night.

Just before I fell asleep, I heard a howl in the distance.

It was a wolf.

I shivered, and closed my eyes.

Chapter Ten

The next morning, we took a vote and decided to stay Up North.

"We just have to be more careful about our hikes," my mom declared. "As long as we don't wander too far from the cabin, we'll be all right. And we can still swim and go to the state park and build campfires."

"And roast marshmallows!" I cried.

So, after breakfast, we drove into town to pick up some supplies. Including marshmallows.

Downtown Fort Deckerville wasn't much to look at. One main street. A gas station. Restaurant. General store. Market. And that was *it*.

We went into the market. It was tiny compared to a full-sized supermarket, but the narrow aisles were crowded with lots of stuff. While my mom filled her basket with all the food on her list, I approached the lady sitting behind the counter. She was skinny and old, but she had a feisty look in her eyes.

"Um, excuse me, ma'am?" I said.

She looked up from a baby blanket she was knitting and smiled.

"The name's Josephine," she said kindly. "What can I do for you, young sir?"

"I was wondering," I began, then glanced at my mom. She was still over by the milk and eggs.

I lowered my voice and continued. "I was wondering if you could tell me anything about Fort Deckerville."

"Well, that's one area where I can be of some service," Josephine said with a chuckle. "I've lived here all my life. We have a population of three hundred seventy-four. No, wait, three hundred seventy-six. I almost forgot about Daisy Tucker, she just had twins. Well, anyhow, our main crops are sugar beets and . . . "

"Um, well, actually," I interrupted, "I wasn't asking about the town. I meant the old fort. Was there anything left after the soldiers burned it down?"

"Ohhh," Josephine clucked. "You're interested in the old legends, are you? Well, I hate to disappoint you, but there's nothing left of the place. At

38

least not up here. I hear they salvaged a cannon and have it on display in a museum down in Detroit."

"Oh, great," I groaned. "You mean more of the fort is back where we came from than where we are now?"

"I'm afraid so," she laughed. "Now if you want to hear some really good stories about the fort, you need to talk to Mr. Jesco Vau- . . . "

"Iggy!" my mom interrupted. "Are you pestering this nice woman?"

"No, Mom," I whined. "I just . . . "

"He's no bother, dear," Josephine insisted. Then a look of concern spread over her face. "Oh, my. Whatever happened to your neck?"

My mom told her about the wolf attack. Josephine was shocked.

"That's terrible!" she said. "Usually, if you don't bother creatures out in the woods, they won't bother you."

"That's what I always heard," my mom said.

"Althoughhhhh," Josephine began, then bit her lip. "No, I shouldn't say anything that might worry you nice folks."

"What?" I cried. My mom shot me a dirty look for being rude to an elder. I added in a more polite voice, "Um, I mean, we'd really like to know what you started to say."

"Well," Josephine began with a smile, "I hate to tell tales. But one of the rumors about that old fort you were just asking me about concerns wolves."

I swallowed hard. "W-wolves?" I asked.

"Mind you, it's just an old story," she said. "But the way some people tell it, one soldier survived the attack on Fort Deckerville. He escaped, and lived long enough to tell people that it wasn't Indians or French settlers who attacked. He said it was . . . wolves. Giant wolves. Like the one you described."

Everyone was silent for a moment. Then Josephine continued, "But of course, that's just a story. Like I said, I've lived here all my life, and I've never seen any wolves, giant, petite or even medium-sized."

"That's right," my mom said, unloading her groceries onto the counter. "You see, boys. They're just old tall-tales."

"But then again," Josephine added, "those woods are deep. You never can tell what they hide. Never can tell."

Chapter Eleven

Back at the cabin, after we unpacked the groceries, Mole and I went outside to play Frisbee.

"Don't wander off too far!" my mom shouted as we bounded out the door.

"That's one thing she doesn't have to worry about," Mole muttered. "I'm not going anywhere near that forest for the rest of this trip."

"Oh, come on, Mole!" I cried. "Didn't that lady at the market make you curious?"

"Curious? Sure," Mole said, flipping the Frisbee to me. "I'd love to know what happened to those soldiers. I just don't want the same thing to happen to me!"

I caught the Frisbee and snapped it back at him.

"I knew all along that was no normal wolf," I said. "The way he was looking at me. He was smarter than an animal."

"What are you saying?" Mole asked, running to catch the Frisbee. He missed and almost tumbled to the ground. I laughed.

He turned beet red and shouted, "D-do you think it was some kind of *monster* wolf?"

I shrugged.

"Who knows?" I said. "Maybe it was a werewolf."

Mole considered what I'd said for a moment. Then he shook his head.

"Nope," he said. "Couldn't be. It was the middle of the day. Werewolves only come out at night. When there's a full moon."

Mole consulted his watch, a wide plastic digital thing with all kinds of extra features.

"And according to my watch," he said, "the next full moon is still two days away."

"Well, it wasn't just a pack of regular old wolves that attacked those soldiers," I said. "It had to be something more."

Mole chucked the Frisbee in my direction.

"The lady said it was just a *story*," he said. "We don't know that wolves had anything to do with it."

Mole's throw was wild and way high. I

jumped to try and snag the Frisbee, but it grazed the tips of my fingers and flew into some bushes behind the outhouse.

"Dag!" I shouted. Then, to Mole, I added, "Nice throw, buddy — if I was seven feet tall!"

"I could've caught it," Mole crowed. "You just need to hustle more."

I snorted and jogged over to the bushes. The Frisbee was nowhere to be seen. I got down on my hands and knees and peered into the brush.

I saw a glimmer of blue plastic.

"Ah, there you are," I grunted, and began to crawl further into the thicket.

Then I heard the growl.

And saw the paws.

Right in front of me.

The wolf was back!

Chapter Twelve

I closed my eyes and screamed, expecting the wolf's jaws to clamp around my throat at any second.

Instead, the next thing I felt was something hot and wet. *Licking* my cheek. A tongue!

Slowly, I opened my eyes. And found myself face-to-face with a cute, slobbery dog.

Before I had a chance to react, Mole came bounding over.

"Iggy!" he shouted. "What happened? I heard you scream!"

Then his face lit up.

"Oh!" he said. "A dog! Hey, puppy. Where'd you come from?"

Mole crouched down and began to play with the dog. Now that I had a better view, I realized that our new friend was much smaller than the wolf. He was a little gray mutt, with matted fur and a crooked left ear.

"Hey there, puppy! Good dog!" Mole said. He glanced in my direction with a grin. "Why'd you scream, anyway? You didn't think this little guy . . . "

"No!" I snapped. "Of course not. I was just, uh, happy. To find the dog."

"A scream of *joy*?" Mole asked, smiling. "Pretty weak, Iggy."

I ignored his comment and started to run back toward the cabin.

"I'm going to ask my mom if we can keep him, at least while we're up here," I shouted over my shoulder. "He doesn't have a tag or a collar."

My mom had been reading a book when Mole and I went out to play. But when I got back inside, the living room was empty.

"Mom!" I called out. "Where are you?"

I poked my head into her bedroom, but it was empty, too. Then I noticed a light in the bathroom.

The door was open, so I walked right in.

My mom was bent over the sink, doing something to her face. It looked like she might be putting on make-up, but I couldn't understand why, when it was the middle of the day and we were in the middle of the woods. But I never could understand the rules of girls and make-up, so I didn't think much of it.

"Hey, Mom, guess what?" I began. "We found a . . . "

Before I could continue, my mom whirled around so fast I jumped back. And she *snarled* at me. Like an animal!

I gasped. She had a crazy look in her eyes. It was like she didn't even recognize me. And her teeth were bared, like she was getting ready to bite.

But most shocking of all was the foam! Her whole face was covered with a thick white lather.

It had to be from the wolf bite!

She was foaming at the mouth!

Chapter Thirteen

In a split-second, it was all over. My mom's eyes softened, and went back to normal. Her mouth curled up in a sad smile. And I realized the foam was actually — shaving cream?

"Oh, hi, Ig. You startled me," my mom said in her sweetest voice. She didn't seem to remember her outburst.

"M- Mom," I stuttered. "W-why . . . why are you ... *shaving?*"

"Oh, this," she laughed, a little nervously. "I, well, this is kind of embarrassing. After we got back from town, I noticed some facial hair. On my cheeks and chin and upper lip."

She ran her fingers through her hair and laughed again.

"This has never happened to me before," she said. "But it's nothing to worry about. Sometimes people's hormones go a little screwy. I'll see Doc Rudolfo when we get back to Detroit."

"So you're not, like, turning into a bearded lady?" I asked.

My mom flicked a glob of shaving cream in my direction. I howled and dashed out of the bathroom.

"I hope not!" she called after me. "But if I do, promise you won't sell me to a circus sideshow?"

"I'll think about it," I responded with a laugh. "Oh, Mom, Mole and I found a stray dog. Can we keep it?"

"No collar? No tags?" she asked. "It's friendly?"

"Nope, nope and yes," I said. "So can we? Can we? Can we?"

"Welllll," she answered. "The next time we go into town, we'll have to ask around and see if anybody lost a dog. But for *now*, I guess it's OK."

"All right!" I yelled. "Thanks, Mom. I promise I'll take care of him."

"We'll have to get some dog food," she said. "But for today, you can feed him some of that ground beef in the fridge."

"OK!" I responded, dashing back into the

kitchen.

I was pretty excited. We'd never been able to have a dog back in Detroit, because our yard was too small and my mom didn't like keeping pets in the house.

When I got back outside with the ground beef, Mole was still wrestling with the puppy.

"What took you so long?" he asked. "I thought you got lost."

"I, uh, my mom was taking a nap," I lied. I didn't want to tell Mole about the shaving incident.

"So?" he asked, scratching the dog's belly. "Can we keep Kaiser Wilhelm?"

"Yeah," I began. "She said — Kaiser Wilhelm! What kind of a name for a dog is that?"

Mole rolled his eyes and sighed loudly.

"Sometimes, Iggy, your ignorance of history shocks even me, your oldest friend," he said. "Don't you get the connection? Kaiser Wilhelm is the *perfect* name for this dog. Let me explain. Well, I guess I'd better start with some background information. If you remember the Battle of . . . "

But as Mole prattled on and Kaiser Wilhelm lapped up his ground beef, my thoughts were elsewhere.

Mole's question about why I took so long reminded me of how weird my mom had acted. What if it did have something to do with the wolf bite? She might have caught rabies, which is supposed to be pretty nasty. The cure has something to do with getting a bunch of shots in the stomach. Ugh.

Then I remembered something Mole and I had talked about earlier. About the mystery of Fort Deckerville.

What if . . . ? Nah. It couldn't be.

I tried to banish the idea from my head. But I couldn't. *What if* those soldiers hadn't been attacked by wolves?

What if they had been attacked by werewolves. What if it had been a werewolf that attacked us?

Then my mom . . .

NO! I told myself firmly. It couldn't be.

Could it?

Chapter Fourteen

That night, the moon was full.

I noticed it around midnight, when I woke up to get a drink of water. The moon was so big and bright it shone through the picture window like some kind of ghostly flashlight.

I ran back up into the loft and shook Mole. He was snoring like a pig.

"Mole! Wake up!" I hissed. "Your crummy watch was wrong! All wrong!"

"Wh-what?" Mole sputtered, rubbing his eyes and reaching for his glasses. "Geez, Iggy, what time is it?"

"It's midnight, and the moon is full!" I barked. "It's full *right now*! Do you know what that means?"

Mole looked sleepy and confused.

"Uh, no, Iggy, I don't," he mumbled. "Who

cares if the moon is full?"

I was going to have to tell Mole my suspicions about my mom.

"Look, Mole, I think something weird is going on," I began. "It has something to do with that wolf that . . . "

Then we heard the howling. It wasn't coming from outside.

It was coming from downstairs.

"The wolf?" Mole cried. "How did it get inside?"

"Th-that's just it," I shouted. The howls grew louder and louder. "I don't think it's the wolf from the other day. I think it's my moth- . . . "

I was interrupted by a horrible cracking sound. The entire loft lurched to one side. Mole tumbled off his bed and landed on top of me. His glasses went flying off the edge.

"What's happening?" he yelled.

"It's the beams," I grunted. "The wooden beams that hold up the loft. Something's tearing them loose."

We heard another crack, and the loft tilted even more violently. A nightstand slid over the edge and crashed to the floor below.

"The window!" I shouted, pointing at a tiny porthole in the far wall. "It's our only chance!"

We clambered to our feet and dashed across the uneven wooden floor. Up close, the window was even smaller than it'd looked.

I grabbed the nearest heavy object — Mole's knapsack full of library books. Using all my strength, I hurled it through the window, smashing out the glass.

"My books!" Mole whined.

"Shut up and get out!" I ordered. "You can pick them up later."

My angry tone seemed to take Mole by surprise. He quickly obeyed me, and started to squeeze through the window.

"Just jump!" I snapped. "The bushes will break your fall—"

I was interrupted by a third crack. This one was the loudest. I felt the floor give way beneath my feet. I felt myself falling!

I landed on my back with a thud. Everything went black for a second. The howling never stopped. It only got louder.

I blinked open my eyes. And screamed.

The wolf from the forest hovered over me.

This time, he stood on his hind legs. His mouth gaped. His teeth glittered like white razors.

Then I realized something strange. He was wearing *clothes*. Familiar-looking clothes. A pair of worn blue jeans. An old Ramones T-shirt. Big silver hoop earrings.

He was a she.

He was . . . my mother!

Chapter Fifteen

"Iggy! Wake up, man! You're dreaming!"

I heard Mole's voice. I felt his hands, shaking me.

I opened my eyes.

And realized I was still lying in bed. The loft was intact. It had all been a dream.

Mole stood over me with a puzzled look on his face.

"You were tossing and turning and moaning," he said. "What were you dreaming about?"

"I don't remember," I lied, rubbing my eyes.

Mole shrugged. "Whatever. I'm going downstairs for breakfast."

I covered my face with a pillow. I didn't want to tell Mole about my nightmare because I didn't want to say something so horrible out loud.

"It was only a dream, Iggy," I whispered to

myself. "There are no such things as werewolves. And even if there were, your mom isn't one!"

A few minutes later, I headed downstairs for breakfast. Mole was working on a heaping plate of bacon and eggs. My mom was standing at the stove, cooking a second batch.

"Morning," I said. "Mmmm. Smells delish."

"It *is*," Mole agreed.

"Yours is coming right up, hon," my mom called.

Suddenly, I felt a whole lot less troubled. The sun was shining through the picture window. A whole new day stretched ahead of us. Breakfast smelled great, and I was famished.

My mom was acting perfectly normal.

What could be better?

"Here you go, Iggy," my mom said, setting a plate down in front of me. "Careful. It's hot."

I immediately began to dig in.

"Aren't you eating, Mom?" I asked through a mouthful of egg.

"Oh, I'm not in the mood for eggs," she responded. "I think I'll just finish up this bacon."

I was busy concentrating on my own breakfast, so I didn't notice anything strange. Until I heard

Mole gagging.

I glanced over in his direction and saw that he'd stopped eating. Mid-bite. A forkful of egg hovered halfway between his plate and his mouth. He had a disgusted look on his face.

"What's wrong with you?" I asked.

Mole silently nodded toward the opposite end of the table.

I turned my head and saw my mom hungrily devouring a plate of bacon.

Raw bacon.

Like an animal, she'd tear off a chunk of one of the fatty strips and gobble it down. Occasionally, she snorted and smacked her lips. She was reading a magazine, so she didn't notice we were staring.

Mole abruptly rose from the table and carried his plate to the sink. My mom glanced up. Half a strip of bacon hung from her mouth. She slurped it up like a spaghetti noodle.

"You done already, John?" she asked through a mouthful of meat.

"Yes, Mrs. Rockwell," Mole murmured. He sounded ill. "I think I'm going to go back upstairs and lie down for awhile."

My mom shrugged. "Suit yourself," she said.

And she casually went back to her meal.

When she took her next bite, the sunlight shone right onto her pearly white teeth.

I gasped. Her teeth were beginning to grow tiny, jagged points!

Chapter Sixteen

After breakfast, Mole and I decided to go for a swim in the lake. By ourselves.

My mom said she didn't feel like coming anyway.

"It's too sunny out," she complained. "I'm just going to stick around here and read."

Mole and I didn't say a word to each other during the entire walk to the lake.

It *was* a sunny day and, by the time we got to the water, we were both good and hot. We left our shirts and shoes in a pile near the edge of the shore and dove in.

Even in the middle of the summer, lakes in Michigan are pretty cold. But today, the shock felt good. I swam as hard as I could all the way out to a diving raft, then back again to the shallows, where Mole was floating on his back. He couldn't swim.

When my feet could finally touch bottom, I

stopped and gasped for breath.

Mole floated over to me and stood up as well. He looked uncomfortable. Like he was embarrassed to talk to me.

Finally, he said, "Um, Iggy? About your mom. Isn't she acting a little weird?"

Without even thinking twice, I blurted out, "I think she's turning into a werewolf!"

Mole's mouth dropped open. It was like I'd just told him that Napoleon had never existed. I could tell that he hadn't even considered the possibility.

"I know it sounds crazy, but it makes sense," I explained. "She got bitten by a wolf. A very strange wolf. Then, yesterday, I caught her shaving."

"Sh-shaving?" Mole stammered.

I nodded solemnly.

"Hair on her face," I said. "And then breakfast this morning. I've never seen her do anything like that before. She doesn't even like *undercooked* meat. She always has to have it well-done. In restaurants, chefs get mad at her, because they say cooking meat well-done ruins it."

Mole gulped.

"Maybe she just has, like, rabies or something?" he said. "If that bite's infected, it could be making her act a little weird."

I put my head in my hands and nodded sadly.

"I thought of that," I said. "So I checked your mini-encyclopedia while you were changing into your swim trunks." Mole always carried a pocket encyclopedia with him, in case he needed to find a fact on the double.

"Rabies doesn't make you do any of that stuff," I said. "I really think she's turning into a werewolf!"

Mole didn't say anything for a moment. Then, quietly, he asked, "Do you know where we could get any silver bullets?"

"What!" I roared. "Are you crazy? We're not shooting my mom with any silver bullets!"

Mole looked scared.

"N-no, Ig, don't take it the wrong way," he said. "I wasn't saying we should shoot your mom. But, you know, a silver bullet might be a good thing to have. In case she stops being your mom and completely turns into a . . . "

I grabbed Mole by the shoulders and shook him savagely.

"Don't even say it!" I cried. "She's not going

to completely turn into a werewolf. There's got to be a way to save her!"

"OK, OK, you're right," Mole whined. A look of pain crossed his face. "Ow, Iggy. You're hurting me."

I realized that I was squeezing Mole's shoulders pretty hard, and let go.

"Sorry, buddy," I sighed. "I'm just scared, that's all."

"It's OK," Mole said. He thought for a moment, then added, "I think we have to confront your mom. Tell her what we suspect. It's for her own good. If we talk to her now, we can get her to a doctor and find out what's wrong."

I dunked my head under the cold water, then looked at Mole and nodded.

"I guess you're right," I said. "I don't know what else to do."

Mole glanced at his plastic wristwatch, which he never removed. Of course, it was waterproof.

"Well, we have to do *something*, and soon," he said glumly. He held out his wrist so I could see the face of the watch.

Only one more day till the moon was full.

Chapter Seventeen

That night, we grilled steaks for dinner and ate at a picnic table in the yard.

My mom insisted on waiting till the sun had almost set before we went out. She only put her steak on the grill for about four seconds.

It was still red and bloody when she cut into it with her knife.

"John! How come you're not eating?" she asked between mouthfuls.

Then she looked at him strangely. Slowly. Up and down.

"We really," she finally said, "need to fatten you up."

Mole's eyes widened, and he turned ghost-white.

My mom smiled and continued, "After all, we don't want your mother to think we starved you up here."

I cleared my throat. I'd been putting off talking to my mom all day. Telling a parent that you think they might be turning into a murderous night creature sure isn't an easy thing to do.

"Uh, Mom?" I began nervously.

"Yes, Iggy?" She looked up at me and grinned.

Her teeth were even pointier. So were the tips of her ears. Thin tufts of dark hair had grown back on her cheeks, her arms, and the back of her hands. Even her eyebrows were joined together in the middle.

This time, she hadn't bothered to shave.

"I was j-just wondering. D-do y-you feel all right?" I asked.

My mom's eyes narrowed into animal-like slits. For a second, it was like I was staring at the wolf!

Then, just as quickly, they softened. She said sweetly, "I'm fine, dear. Why do you ask? Don't I *seem* all right?"

I took a quick gulp of Faygo Red Pop. Before I could respond, Mole jumped in.

"I think Iggy's just worried about that bite on your neck, Mrs. Rockwell," he said in his politest voice. "Maybe you should get it checked out."

My mom laughed, a little too loud. It was more of a bark then a laugh. Mole and I jumped in our seats.

"It's sweet of you two to worry about me," she began, still smiling. Then, without any warning, her face twisted into a hideous snarl.

"BUT I SAID I WAS FINE!" she roared. Spit flew out of her mouth. I thought she was going to attack. "AND THAT'S THE LAST I WANT TO HEAR ABOUT IT!"

I was too startled to move. Mole was frozen in his seat, too.

Then, just as suddenly, the old Mom was back again. And she didn't remember a thing.

"So!" she said cheerfully. "Why so quiet, boys? And who's ready for some dessert?"

"I-I'll have a cup of coffee, Mom," I murmured.

"Coffee?" she asked, wrinkling her nose. "You don't drink coffee. Besides, you'll be up all night."

"That's the idea," I muttered under my breath, staring up at the moon that was just beginning to appear. The moon that was only one day away from being full.

It was going to be a long night.

Chapter Eighteen

"We need a new plan," Mole whispered.

It was almost midnight. We were back up in the loft, sitting cross-legged on the floor. Our only light was a flickering candle. It cast huge, dark shadows on the walls and made everything kind of spooky.

I nodded in agreement.

"Let's go over our options," I said. "We've got no phone, so we can't call for help."

"Right," Mole said. "It's too far to walk to town, isn't it?"

"Yeah," I admitted glumly. "And there are no neighbors for miles."

"We could start a signal fire," Mole suggested. "Maybe we'd attract a plane flying overhead."

"This isn't *Gilligan's Island*," I groused.

"How many planes fly over Fort Deckerville?"

"I don't know," Mole shot back. "I'm just trying to help. Maybe we should just start walking. We'd get somewhere eventually."

"I don't want to abandon my mom, though," I said.

"We could tie her up," Mole offered. "It'd be for her own good."

Before I could tell Mole to shut up, the howls began.

This time, it was no dream.

They came from outside. From the forest. A chorus of yelps and whoops and growls.

"Th-that sounds like more than just a couple," Mole stammered.

"It's probably the moon," I said. "Probably the closer it comes to full, the wilder the wolves get."

Suddenly, from down below, we heard the bedroom door open.

"Quick, blow out the candle!" Mole whispered furiously. "It's your mom!"

I puffed out the flame and we sat perfectly still. Waiting. Listening. I tried not to breathe. Staring across at Mole, I could see him shivering in the gloom.

We heard footsteps cross the living room floor.

We heard the front door slowly creak open. And slam shut.

Then we heard a new howl. It came from just below the loft window.

I couldn't resist. I dashed over to the window and pressed my face against the glass. It was cold to the touch.

Down below, I saw my mother.

She was wearing her nightshirt.

She was crouching on all fours.

She was baying at the moon.

Then, in a flash, she bounded off into the woods.

And she was gone.

Chapter Nineteen

We tried to stay up all night and wait for my mom to come back.

But Mole fell asleep around two in the morning. And I must have drifted off shortly after that.

I woke up the next morning to the sound of birds twittering outside our window. Mole was curled up on the floor, snoring loudly. I rubbed my eyes, then kicked him in the back with a bare foot.

"Huh? What?" he grunted. He sat up and looked around. "Oh. Hey."

He paused, then asked quietly, "So, is she back yet?"

"I don't know," I responded. My stomach churned nervously. "But we'd better go down and find out."

The first thing we noticed when we got downstairs was the front door. It was wide open.

"Lucky we're not still in the city," Mole whispered. "Anybody could've walked in."

I nodded, and looked around the living room. Nothing was messed up. Everything seemed to be in order. The door to my mom's room was closed.

"I guess I'd better check on her," I said. "Why don't you look around outside and make sure everything's OK."

"Right," Mole agreed. He paused before going outside, then added, "And, uh, Iggy? Be careful."

I started to get mad again.

"We're talking about my mom, not some kind of wild animal," I said. "She's not danger- . . . "

"I know!" Mole interrupted, then quickly lowered his voice. "I know," he repeated. "I just — well, we don't really know *what* she's going to do next, do we?"

"No," I admitted softly. "You're right, Mole. I'm sorry. Thanks. I'll be careful."

He nodded and stepped outside. I swallowed and turned to face the closed bedroom door.

All along, I'd been hoping that this whole werewolf thing had been a figment of my imagination. But last night, I had see it with my own eyes.

Now I was wondering if my mom could ever

be saved. I'll have to be firm with her, I told myself.

I'll just say: Mom, you're sick. We need to get you to town. To a doctor.

But deep in my heart, I doubted a doctor would know how to treat a werewolf. What if they decided to keep her locked up? Or worse?

I took a deep breath and slowly opened the door to her bedroom.

The first thing I noticed was the smell. My mom's room at home smells great. It's a mixture of perfume and incense and the fancy soap she gets at the Body Barn.

But this room smelled horrible. Like a wet dog. Like a moldy forest. Like spoiled meat.

I grimaced and tried not to breathe through my nose. The room was completely dark. All the shades were drawn. I squinted into the gloom and could barely make out a shape on the bed.

"M-Mom?" I stammered, softly at first, then louder. "I-is that you?"

No response.

I waited for a moment, then slowly made my way toward the bed.

The shape on top was covered with sheets. They were tangled and messy. It looked like she'd been tossing and turning all night.

Well, not *all* night, obviously. But for as long as she'd been home. Maybe the side effect of being a werewolf is that you have really bad dreams.

"Mom?" I murmured again.

Still no answer.

I held my breath. Slowly, I reached down and touched the edge of the sheet. She didn't move.

With a single, quick movement, I pulled back the sheet.

And discovered a pillow.

That was it.

I breathed again. But I wasn't relieved. Not totally.

I had expected to see the worst. A fur-covered wolf-mom. But not seeing *anything* was almost as bad. That meant she'd never come home. Where could she be?

I imagined her lost in the woods. The forest was huge! Or hurt somewhere, with a twisted ankle. Or attacked by some wild animal. Or . . .

Then I heard the bedroom door slam closed behind me.

The light from the living room was shut out, and with the window shades still drawn, the whole room suddenly went pitch black.

I felt a hand grip my shoulder. Long, sharp fingernails dug into my flesh.

And I let out a scream of terror!

Chapter Twenty

Not that my scream did much good.

Another hand quickly covered my mouth. I could taste the thick fur covering the palm.

A voice whispered in my ear. Familiar, yet raspy. It was definitely my mom. But she didn't sound good. Not good at all.

"Son?" she purred. She seemed to be talking from the back of her throat. Growling. "What are you doing, snooping around in your mommy's room? Didn't I teach you it's not nice to snoop?"

I couldn't talk. Mostly because I was too scared. But also because her hand was still tightly clamped over my mouth. I just nodded in agreement. Her hand smelled like the woods.

"I haven't been feeling so well," she continued. "I'm not sure what's wrong with me. But I didn't get much sleep last night. So I'd appreciate it if you and your little friend left me alone today. No noise. No rough-housing. No bothering me for lunch or playing or driving you to town. Do you understand?"

I nodded again. The more she talked, the angrier she sounded. Her grip on my shoulder tightened. I could feel her nails — not nails, *claws* — piercing my thin T-shirt. Beginning to pierce my *skin*.

"Good," she hissed. "I'm glad we understand each other. Now go tell your friend. And don't make me repeat myself."

Without warning, I felt myself being lifted off the floor.

Now, I realize that I'm still a growing boy. But I'm not tiny. And my mom's not huge. Or a body builder.

But she picked me up like I was a newborn baby. Or like she was Arnold Schwarzennegger.

In a flash, the bedroom door opened. And then I went flying through the air, back out into the living room.

Before I landed, though, I managed to glance over my shoulder. Standing in the bedroom door, I caught a glimpse of my mom. You could still tell it was my mom.

But thicker patches of brown fur covered her face and her hands. And the hair on her head had grown longer.

The other thing I noticed was that she was smiling. With her mouth open. A mouth full of fangs.

Then the door slammed shut. And I crashed onto the floor in a heap.

Chapter Twenty-One

"Uhh," I moaned.

My head ached. My shoulder throbbed. And my mom was even worse off than I could've possibly imagined in my scariest daydreams!

I pulled myself to my feet and shook my head, then stumbled into the kitchen. My shoulder was bleeding a bit from where my mom had scratched me. I grabbed some paper towels off a big roll and turned up my shirt sleeve.

I wrapped the cuts as tightly as I could, without cutting off the circulation. There wasn't a lot of blood, so I didn't worry much about myself.

After I was finished with the bandaging, I still had the taste of fur in my mouth, so I went to the sink and got a glass of water. And tried to think straight.

"OK, Iggy, just stay calm," I told myself. "There's gotta be a way out of this."

But the full moon was coming *tonight*!

I glanced at the clock on the kitchen wall. Five minutes to noon. We had about eight hours before nightfall.

Eight hours before my mom's horrible transformation would be complete.

I ran my fingers through my hair and tried to come up with a new plan. I tried to remember everything I could about werewolves. Unfortunately, most of what I knew about werewolves came from comic books and dumb horror movies.

Let's see, does garlic . . . ? No. That's vampires.

Running water? Ditto.

How *was* a guy supposed to stop a werewolf, without having to shoot it with a silver bullet?

My thoughts were interrupted by a scream.

It was coming from outside.

It was Mole!

Chapter Twenty-Two

I ran outside and saw Mole standing next to a tree. He was holding his head in his hands.

"Nooooo!" he cried as I dashed over. "I can't believe it! This couldn't have happened! I *won't* believe it!"

"Mole, what's the matter?" I asked breathlessly. "What are you screaming about?"

Mole whirled around and shouted, "*This* is what's the matter! Look!"

He held up a tattered dog collar. It was made of thick leather. But someone — some*thing* — had ripped it in half like a ticket stub.

It was Kaiser Wilhelm's collar. We'd just bought it the day before. He'd been tied to the tree Mole was standing next to.

Now, he was nowhere to be seen.

"He's gone," Mole whimpered. "I've been calling him for five minutes. Do you think . . . do you think she could've ... "

I didn't want to think about it. But after what'd happened in the bedroom, I knew anything was possible.

Sadly, I nodded my head, and told Mole about my encounter with my mom.

"We've got to do something," I said. "And fast. By the time the sun sets and the moon comes out, it might be too late to save her."

"OK. But first, I want to bury this," Mole said, staring at the collar. "It's the least we could do for the poor little guy."

"We really don't have the time," I started to argue.

But Mole snapped, "It's all that's left of Kaiser Wilhelm! It wouldn't be proper to just forget about him. Try and show a little bit of respect, please!"

I sighed. Mole could be pretty stubborn when it came to old-fashioned honor and being "proper" and other things he'd read about in history books. I figured it would be faster to humor him rather than sit and argue for ten minutes.

Plus, we needed time to decide on our next move.

"All right," I said. "Maybe there's a shovel in the cellar. Mr. Vincent said there were some old tools down there we could use if we wanted to. Let's go check. The sooner we get this over with, the sooner we can come up with a plan to help my mother."

The entrance to the cellar was in back of the cabin. A pair of wooden doors opened up in the ground at a slight angle. A musty odor wafted up from below when we pulled open the creaky old doors. Ugh! It didn't look like anyone had been down below the house in ages.

Clammy stone steps led down into the darkness.

"Well," I said, as we stared down into the pit, "if there's a shovel, it should be down there somewhere."

"I-if you think you know where it is, maybe you should get it," Mole suggested. "It'd save time, after all, and we are in a pretty big hurry."

"No way!" I shouted. "You wanna bury that stupid collar, you're getting the shovel. I'm not going down there. No way, no how, uh-uh."

"Well, I think we should at least flip a coin then," Mole whined. "That's the only fair way to resolve our difference of opin- . . . "

"No!" I shouted. "I'm not flipping any . . . "

A door slammed, interrupting our argument.

The front door of the cabin.

We stopped and listened as footsteps approached. Then my mother rounded the corner of the cabin and stood before us.

Even though it was a hot summer morning, she was wearing her jeans and combat boots and black leather jacket. She had the jacket zipped tight, right up to her neck.

She had also put on my Detroit Tigers baseball cap. It was pulled down low on her head. The bill shadowed much of her face. She was wearing sunglasses.

Mole dropped the dog collar. His legs started shaking.

"Iggy!" she barked. Her voice sounded even worse than it did only five minutes before. "Didn't I just ask you for some peace and quiet?"

I don't know how I was able to speak, but somehow, I said, "Y-yes, Mom."

"Well, then," she snarled, "why did I just hear someone *screaming*! At the top of their little lungs! Right outside my window! While I was trying to sleep!"

She took another step toward us. I got a better look at the thick fur covering her hands. I saw the pointy, gnarled claws at the ends of her fingers.

Mole spoke in a shaky voice.

"Th- that was me, Mrs. Rockwell," he said. "I'm very sorry. I didn't realize you were resting. It won't happen again. I promise. R-really."

"It's too late for apologies, *Mole*," she spat, taking another step forward.

Uh-oh, I thought. She *never* calls John by his nickname, not on purpose like that.

"You've been a very bad boy!" she yelled. "And now, you have to be punished!"

And with a blood-curdling roar, she leapt straight toward us!

Chapter Twenty-Three

I couldn't move. I stood frozen in place. Waiting to be devoured by my own mother!

To my right, I heard Mole's voice crying, "Iggy! Hit the dirt!"

I felt myself being tackled to the ground — not by my mom, but by Mole. As we crashed onto the grass, I saw a blur whiz right over us.

Then I heard a crash. And a howl of rage.

"Quick, Iggy!" Mole shouted, scrambling to his feet. "She landed in the cellar! Help me bolt it shut!"

I was too confused to react. After all, we were talking about my mom. When was the last time you discussed bolting one of *your* parents in the cellar?

"A-are you sure she's not hurt?" I asked weakly.

"She's fine!" Mole huffed as he slammed the wooden cellar doors shut. "Can't you hear her?"

Sure enough, I heard a horrible growling coming from down below. And the sound of feet scurrying up the cellar steps.

"Quick," Mole shouted, "help me lock these down!"

He was leaning with all his weight on the doors. But since we're talking about Mole, a fairly skinny guy, we're not talking about much weight at all.

A thick padlock rested on a ledge a few feet away. Mr. Vincent only locked the doors if nobody was renting his cabin and it would be empty for a few weeks.

I dashed over and grabbed the lock. Before I could hand it to Mole, something slammed against the bottom of the cellar doors with a loud crash.

Mole almost fell over backwards. The doors cracked open. A hairy, gnarled fist emerged.

And grabbed Mole by the wrist!

"Iggy!" he cried, sobbing with pain. "She's got me!"

Chapter Twenty-Four

I hesitated for a second.

Mole cried out again.

"Iggy! Help!" he yelled. "Do something! Hurry!"

I gritted my teeth.

"Sorry, Mom," I whispered. Then, with all my might, I slammed the heavy padlock down on her twisted paw.

A savage howl echoed from down below. The hand recoiled. And opened up, releasing Mole.

With a final shove, we forced the cellar doors closed. I leaned forward and snapped the lock shut.

The howling continued. The doors shook. We heard her fists pounding at her prison. The thick, old, wooden doors rattled and creaked, but didn't break.

We were safe.

I stepped away from the cellar doors and glanced at Mole. He'd backed off, too, and looked pretty rattled.

"You OK?" I asked, wiping my brow. For a few moments there, I had thought Mole was going to end up one arm short.

Mole nodded as he rubbed his wrist.

"I'm fine," he said. "Your mom has quite a grip, though. But the real question is, what do we do now?"

Before I could answer, I was interrupted by a familiar voice.

"Iggggy!" It was my mom. Her voice sounded almost *normal* again, coming from the other side of the doors. Normal, and sad.

"Son, why are you doing this to me?" my mom called. "Please, let me out. I'm hurt. I-I think I twisted my leg. It might be broken. And it's dark down here. I'm scared. I need help."

I swallowed hard and, even though I knew better, I started having second thoughts. I looked at Mole.

"No way," he said flatly. "I'm sorry, Iggy, but we just can't do it. It's too dangerous. She almost ripped my arm off!"

"I heard that, Mole, you little fink!" roared the voice from below. It no longer sounded like my mom. It had all been an act! "And after I invited you along on this vacation! You'll be sorry when I get out. You hear me? You'll both be very sorry!"

The doors started to shake again as she pounded and pounded. Mole looked scared. I tried to shut out her voice. But I couldn't.

"Come on, Mole," I said. "Let's get outta here. I can't take any more of this. We've gotta do something."

"Where are we going?" he asked, still staring nervously at the cellar doors as we walked away from the cabin.

"To town," I said firmly, trying to sound sure of myself, although, deep down, I felt pretty scared. "To get help."

After a pause, I added, "We're taking the van."

Chapter Twenty-Five

"Make sure you fasten your seat belt," I told Mole.

He slid into the passenger seat next to me. He looked pretty nervous.

I felt pretty nervous myself. I'd never driven before, other than go-carts and Indy 500 arcade games where, if you crash, you either bump into a rubber wall or just plop in another token.

"You sure we shouldn't just walk?" Mole asked.

"No time," I said, sliding my seat all the way forward. "We'll be fine. How hard can this be?" I was actually trying to convince myself more than Mole.

Mole didn't answer.

I sneered at him and said, "Thanks for all the support."

Then I took a deep breath. And turned the

ignition key. The van's engine started up immediately.

"I think you have to step on the brake before you put her in gear," Mole offered.

"I know!" I snapped. Actually, I hadn't known. But I didn't want *Mole* to know that.

I stepped on the brake and slid the lever on the side of the steering wheel until it lined up with "D" — Drive. Easy enough. Piece of cake, in fact. Then I eased up on the brake.

Slowly, verrry slowly, the van started to roll forward.

"Watch out for that tree!" Mole shouted. The nearest tree was about thirty feet away.

"Don't worry, Mole," I insisted, even though my knuckles were white from gripping the steering wheel so tightly. "This isn't that hard."

To my surprise, it wasn't. I was kind of enjoying myself. Well, as much as I possibly could, considering I'd just left my half-werewolf mother locked in a cellar.

I tried not to step on the gas much, so the van didn't go too fast. Keeping the steering wheel steady was no problem. All those driving video games really weren't a waste of time after all. And, of course, traffic wasn't something I had to worry about in Fort Deckerville.

Now, there was only one problem: Where *were* we, anyway?

Whenever my mom drove, I didn't pay much attention to directions. But now I wished I'd paid more attention when we drove to town. Especially since we were out in the boonies. Where all the unpaved, tree-lined streets looked alike. And there were no street signs.

"Are you lost?" Mole asked. We'd been driving around for about ten minutes. It was a reasonable question, I'll admit.

"No!" I shouted. "At least, I don't think so. I'm pretty sure we're going in the right direction. Roughly."

"*Roughly*," Mole spat. He shook his head with disgust and looked away from me, out the passenger-side window. "I can't believe I ever listened to you. We're hopelessly lost. In the middle of nowhere. No phone, no food, half a tank of gas. We'll probably run out of gas and get eaten by a bear! You're such an idiot!"

That was the last straw. I couldn't take it anymore. My face flushed.

"*I'm* an idiot?" I shouted, whirling around to face Mole. "Maybe I can't tell you the date the War of 1812 ended, or who signed the treaty, or what countries even fought in the stupid thing! But I sure didn't hear any better ideas coming from you! So unless you've got something positive to say, I'd appreciate it if you kept your nasty comments to yourself!"

A look of horror passed over Mole's face.

Geez, I thought, pleased with myself. I must have sounded pretty tough. I should stand up for myself more often.

"Iggy!" Mole finally cried. "The road! Look out!"

"Oh no!" I thought. I whipped my head back toward the windshield.

Just in time to see us careening straight toward a huge oak tree!

<u>Chapter Twenty-Six</u>

I wrenched the steering wheel as hard as I could and stomped on the brakes. The van sailed off the road, barely missing the tree before crashing to a halt against a fallen log.

My head jerked forward and almost hit the steering wheel. Luckily, the seat belt locked up and held me in place.

Then everything was perfectly still.

I looked over at Mole. He stared back at me with a slightly dazed look on his face.

"You OK?" he asked weakly.

I nodded.

"I don't think this van is, though," I said. The engine had died after our crash. I tried turning the key again, but nothing happened. Not even a sputter.

"Guess we're walking," Mole sighed.

We climbed out of the van and checked out the damage. It was pretty bad. The front end was crushed against the log. The hood had popped open a little bit, and steam was pouring out of the engine area.

"Guess you're right," I said, feeling more depressed than ever. "I really am an idiot."

"No, I didn't mean it, Iggy," Mole protested, grabbing my arm. "Everything has just, you know, been kind of tense. Scary. I don't have any better ideas. You've been doing your best."

I sat down and put my head in my hands.

"Yeah, and that's just not good enough," I moaned. "We're lost in the woods, in the middle of nowhere, with no idea of which way to walk. And in a few hours, my mom will turn into a bloodthirsty creature of the night!"

"We can still save her, Iggy," Mole insisted. "There's still plenty of time. Well, not *plenty*. But there's still time. We just have to keep trying."

I looked up at Mole and immediately felt better.

"You're right," I said, springing to my feet. "We can't give up. My mom's depending on us, even if she doesn't know it. We're both young, strong, smart. We've gotta come up with something. If we stick together, nothing can stop us!"

Just as my speech ended, we heard a click coming from the woods behind us.

The click of a rifle being cocked.

"Now don't either of y'all move a muscle, y'hear," drawled a deep, country voice. "Or I'll blow you away without thinkin' twice."

Chapter Twenty-Seven

"P-please, d-don't shoot us," I stammered.

The voice didn't respond. I closed my eyes and braced for the worst. I heard footsteps crunching on the ground in front of me.

Slowly, I opened my eyes again. And saw a grown man, about my mom's age, but only a little bit taller than me. He was pointing a very deadly-looking rifle at my belly.

But the funny thing was, even with his gun, the guy didn't look all that tough.

First of all, like I said, he was pretty short for an adult. He had messy black hair and beard stubble on his face, and he squinted at me from behind a thick pair of glasses. It looked like he had robbed a thrift store for his weird, mismatched outfit: green Army camouflage pants, a purple polo shirt, sandals and a floppy fishing cap.

And *he* looked more scared than I felt. The

gun was shaking a little bit. His lower lip trembled.

"I heard the crash," he finally said, gesturing toward the van with his head. "Where did you two come from?"

"Detroit. But we were staying in a cabin somewhere back that way," I explained, pointing down the road where we'd come from.

"I told you not to move!" the man shouted. His eyes bugged out and his voice cracked a bit. Beads of sweat ran down his face.

"S-sorry, sir," I whimpered. "Calm down. Please. Don't shoot."

"You still didn't explain what you're doing out in this neck of the woods," he snapped. "And who was driving that van? You both look too young to have licenses. You out for a joy-ride? Huh? Answer me! You boys out for trouble?"

"No!" I said. "My mom's, um, sick. We took the van to get help. We got lost. Then we ran off the road. It was my fault. It was my first time driving."

"Hmm," the man snorted. He squinted at us for a few more moments, trying to look mean. Finally, his face fell, and he stopped pointing the rifle at us.

"All right," he sighed. "I'm sorry if I scared

you. I'm just not used to getting unexpected visitors, that's all. I'm not used to getting *any* visitors, to tell you the truth, not in this neck of the woods. It's usually just me and the squirrels and the trees."

Mole and I breathed sighs of relief. The stranger extended his hand. "The name's Jesco," he said. "Jesco Vaughn."

"I'm Iggy, and this is my friend John," I said, shaking his hand. He had a weak, sweaty grip. After we shook, I wiped my hand on my shorts when he wasn't looking.

"So, um, Jesco," Mole began, "if you don't mind my asking, what happened to your Southern accent?"

"Oh, that," Jesco laughed nervously. "I just did that to scare you guys. To sound tough." He laughed again. Jesco's real voice was kind of squeaky.

"I've been living out in these parts for about twenty years now," he continued. "I'm a writer. I decided to move away from the city so I could get more work done. There are fewer distractions out here. Unless you like talking to acorns."

"What kind of stuff do you write about?" I asked. I really wanted to start figuring out what to do about my mom. But he was still holding the gun, so I thought I'd better be polite.

"What do I write about?" he repeated, laughing harshly. "You wouldn't understand, kid. Nobody understands. That's why I have to be careful about who comes near my property. There's a lot of people who are working against me. Who don't want to see my research completed."

Oh no, I thought. We're trapped in the woods with a half-crazy, paranoid hermit. I shot a glance at Mole. He rolled his eyes.

"I study things science can't explain," Jesco continued. He stared at the sky and pointed. "Things from out there." He looked at the ground and pointed again. "Things from below." He stared at us. "Things you'd never believe in, kid. Not in a million years."

I gulped, then said, in a shaky voice, "Things like, oh, I don't know — werewolves?"

Jesco turned as white as a ghost.

"What do you know about werewolves?" he whispered, leaning close to me. From the way his breath smelled, it didn't seem likely he kept a toothbrush out here in the woods. "Huh? Who's been talking to you about werewolves, kid? What are you two really up to?"

"My mom," I said. "She was bitten by a wolf the other day. Not a regular wolf. Bigger. Smarter. And since then, she's been changing. She's in a bad way. We don't know what to do."

"What are the symptoms?" Jesco asked. I told him. He turned even whiter and sat down on a stump. "Tonight's the full moon," he murmured.

"We know!" I cried. "That's why we took the van. We were looking for help. And you're the perfect helper. You're an expert on weird things! Is there a cure? Come on! You must know!"

Jesco shook his head slowly. "Werewolves aren't my specialty. I deal with UFOs. Vampires. The Native American spirit world. The occasional ghost story. All I know about werewolves . . . "

He stopped.

"What?" I shouted. "Tell us, Jesco. We're running out of time! Please! You're the only chance we've got!"

"Well," he said, scratching his head, "I had an old girlfriend who was into werewolves. She believed it was werewolves that killed all those soldiers in Fort Deckerville, so she was living up in these parts for awhile, studying the area. Left me, though. Said I didn't bathe enough. But I take baths! I do! I . . . "

"Jesco!" I interrupted. "Please! Stick to what you know about werewolves!"

"Sorry," he said. "Anyway, just from having this girlfriend who was a werewolf buff and all, I learned bits and pieces here and there. I've forgotten most of it. Like I said, not my area of interest. And what I'm about to tell you, we'll have to double-check in a book I have. But, from what I remember, the only way to save a person once they've been bitten — well, it's just impossible."

He paused for a moment, then continued. "To save your mom, we need one thing."

"What is it?" I asked frantically. "Tell us! Please!"

"The wolf," he said grimly. "We need to find the wolf that bit her."

Chapter Twenty-Eight

Jesco's place, not surprisingly, was a dump.

He lived far back from the road, in a large, wooden cabin that was hidden behind a cluster of trees. He took us there to find a book.

"It's a book about werewolves, and I'm pretty sure it explains the cure," he explained, as he led us into his library. Books were stacked on tables, on chairs, on the floor — everywhere but in the shelves where they belonged.

"What does it look like?" Mole asked.

"It's either green or brown," Jesco responded. "I think. Or maybe a dark red. Or black."

I sighed. "So what you're saying is, we should just look for a book that says, 'WEREWOLVES.' "

"Actually," Jesco explained, "it's in Latin, so you won't be able to read the title. But don't worry. I think I know exactly where it is."

Fifteen minutes later, Jesco was still rifling through pile after pile of books. I sat in a stuffed chair and tapped my foot nervously. Mole was examining an old skull. A human skull.

"I *bought* that, I just want you to know," Jesco called out while he searched. Then, with a shout, he sprang to his feet. "Aha! Here it is!"

We dashed over and crowded around the book he held. For the record, it was blue.

"All right," he murmured as he flipped through the book. "Cure, cure, cure . . . Where is that cure? Ah! Here we go!"

The thin, yellowed page was covered, top to bottom, with tiny Latin text.

"What does it say?" I cried.

Jesco frowned.

"I'm afraid I was correct," he muttered. "To save your mother, we have to get her to drink a strange concoction. One part water."

"We can get that," Mole said.

"Yes," Jesco continued, "but the second ingredient is more difficult. We need some fur." He looked up at us. "From the wolf that bit her."

I moaned. "How will we ever find that same wolf?"

Jesco looked out a nearby window. The sun would be up for a few more hours.

"He'll be out," Jesco said grimly. "There's a full moon tonight. That drives them crazy. He'll find *you*."

I swallowed hard. My knees started to shake at the thought of meeting that wolf again. But I had to find him. I had to save my mom.

"Can you help us, Jesco?" I asked. "You know these woods. And you've got your rifle."

Jesco laughed. "*That* gun? It's not loaded. I never bought any bullets for it. I'm scared of guns. I just keep it around to scare people."

My heart sank. Now it was *really* hopeless. But Jesco smiled and continued.

"You're right, though," he said. "I *do* know these woods. Let's go find us a wolf."

Chapter Twenty-Nine

Jesco didn't have a car. He didn't even have a driver's license. So we walked.

And walked. And walked.

We saw squirrels and birds and a glimpse of a deer. But not a single wolf.

"Are you sure *they'll* find *us*?" I asked Jesco. We'd been wandering around the woods for a few hours. The sun was starting to set.

He leaned against a tree and wiped his sweaty brow.

"Like I said, I'm not a werewolf expert," he said. "I can only tell you what I've heard and read. I've lived up here for a long time. But I've never seen a werewolf. Most of the people who live in Fort Deckerville have never even seen a regular old wild wolf. Why do you think that is?"

Mole and I both shrugged at the same time.

"Because werewolves only show themselves

to people they *want*," he continued. "To victims. And if my hunch is right, the wolf that bit Iggy's mother *really* wanted Iggy."

I shivered.

Mole asked, "Why would a bunch of werewolves decide to attack the old fort in the first place?"

"Well, according to the legend, the soldiers were stationed up here for a while," Jesco explained. "And if you think there's nothing to do in Fort Deckerville *now*, imagine what it was like two hundred years ago. When soldiers aren't fighting, they get antsy. So these soldiers decided to go hunting. And since they were soldiers, they decided to hunt the most powerful creature in the forest."

"The wolf," I said.

"Give that young man a cigar," Jesco grinned. "Yes. You're correct. They went out into the forest and slaughtered a bunch of wolves. Not to eat the meat, of course. Just for sport. They left the carcasses scattered throughout the woods. And — according to the legend — the wolves decided to get even."

"That's when they attacked the fort?" Mole asked.

"Right," Jesco said. "And since then, according to the legend, whenever someone in town has been bitten by a wolf, they've — well, they've started acting weird. Like your mother, Iggy."

"And once the full moon comes out?" I asked.

Jesco looked down at his feet and said quietly, "It's not like in the movies, where once a month, when the moon is full, you need a shave. These people really turned into wolves. Like the one you saw in the woods the other day. They were never seen again."

"You mean," I stammered, "after this first full moon, my mom will *stay* a werewolf? Forever?"

Jesco looked up.

"I don't know," he said. "That's just how the stories go. Like I said, I've never even *seen* a werewolf, let alone . . . "

Just then, we heard a crash in the forest behind us. We whirled around.

Standing there, snarling and drooling and baring his razor-sharp teeth, was a wolf.

The wolf.

My wolf.

"Well, guess I spoke too soon, boys," Jesco

whispered. "*Now* I've seen one."

With a savage roar, the wolf leaped forward and attacked.

Chapter Thirty

Jesco was right about one thing. The wolf was after *me*.

I managed to let out a scream. Then his front paws slammed into my chest. I felt his hot breath on my face again. I fell backwards onto the ground.

For a split second, time stopped. I saw the wolf's head, hovering above me. I stared right into his gaping mouth. Into his evil yellow eyes.

For a split second, he seemed to smile.

Then Jesco launched our plan.

According to his werewolf book, if we wanted to save my mom, we couldn't *kill* the wolf that bit her. And since Jesco didn't even have bullets for his gun, that wasn't an option anyway.

Jesco *did* have ammunition for another weapon, though. It was a South American blow gun he'd picked up at a flea market many years earlier. It was basically a long tube you loaded with little darts. You blow on one end, the darts fly out the other.

"These darts'll knock out an elephant," Jesco had told us back at the cabin. "At least, that's what the guy at the flea market said."

"You mean you've never tested them out?" Mole had cried.

Jesco had shrugged and smiled. "There's no time like the present."

The wolf was getting ready to chomp on me when Jesco sent the dart sailing. I saw it fly over my face. It hit the wolf dead in the neck. He howled and jumped back.

I felt arms pull me to my feet and away from the wolf. It was Mole. I glanced at Jesco. He was still clutching his blow gun, looking nervous.

We all turned to watch the wolf. He looked like a dog chasing his tail. He was trying to nip at the dart, still stuck in his neck. But he couldn't reach it.

"Pretty good shot, eh?" Jesco grinned.

"Don't pat yourself on the back too soon," Mole cautioned. "Look!"

The wolf had stopped spinning around, trying to get at the dart. He stood in the middle of the road, on wobbly legs, not moving.

Then he looked up. At Jesco.

"I thought you said he'd be out cold by now," I hissed.

"It's not working," Jesco stammered. "I don't know why."

A rumbling growl started in the back of the wolf's throat. White foam bubbled from the edges of his massive jaws.

He's not fooling around anymore, I thought. This time, we're dead!

Chapter Thirty-One

The wolf crouched down and prepared to pounce.

Jesco fumbled with his blow gun and another dart. Mole began to shake wildly. I took a step back without even thinking.

The wolf leaped into the air, straight for Jesco.

And, just before impact, crashed into the dirt. Out cold.

Nobody said anything for a moment. Then Mole whispered, "I think the dart kicked in."

Slowly, carefully, Jesco took a step forward and gave the wolf a slight kick. Not a twitch. Not a stir.

I breathed a sigh of relief. "That was close."

"Too close," Jesco agreed. He crouched next to the wolf. Reaching into his pocket, he removed a pair of scissors and a vial of water. He leaned forward and clipped off a tiny clump of the wolf's fur.

"That's all we need?" I asked.

"According to my recipe," Jesco responded. He dropped the fur into the water and shook the vial until it was blended. No smoke or bubbles magically appeared. It just looked like soggy bits of fur in a vial of water.

"I hope this works," I said, my voice trembling.

Jesco looked up at the sky. The sun had almost set. Soon, the moon would be out.

The full moon.

We didn't have much time.

"Come on, Iggy," Jesco said, his voice shaking, too. "It's time to find your mother."

Chapter Thirty-Two

It took us about twenty minutes to find the cabin. Jesco knew the woods like a scout. When we told him it was Mr. Vincent's place, he knew exactly what we were talking about.

As we walked up the gravel driveway, the first thing I noticed was how deserted the place looked. The van was gone. The cabin was dark. And, of course, there were no streetlights around to make us feel any safer.

"Where is she?" Jesco whispered.

I pointed toward the back of the cabin. "In the cellar. The door's back that way."

Slowly, we marched toward the back of the cabin.

"Hopefully, Iggy, you'll be able to convince her to drink our little potion," Jesco said. "But if she's too far gone, we'll just do the same thing we did out there in the woods. I'll hit her with a dart."

He handed me the vial. "And when she goes down, you pour this down her throat."

"What about me?" Mole asked.

"Hopefully, you won't have to do anything," Jesco replied. "But just be ready to jump in and back us up."

As we neared the cellar doors, I tripped over something in the grass. I stooped down and saw the padlock.

Broken.

I looked up and saw Mole and Jesco standing perfectly still. The doors were smashed open.

I looked even higher and saw the full moon. It had risen.

My mom had escaped.

Chapter Thirty-Three

"Oh no!" I cried. "We're too late!"

"Maybe not," Mole said, crouching in front of the doors. "Look. Footprints. They seem pretty fresh."

From the shape of the prints, it looked like my mom was still wearing her boots.

She must've escaped before her feet turned into paws, I thought grimly.

"Well," I said aloud, "we'd better follow the prints before she hurts somebody. It looks like they're heading into the woods."

Jesco grimaced. "The only problem is, we won't be able to follow this trail for long. Not in this darkness. Once we get under the trees, we won't even have the moonlight to see by."

"I think there's a flashlight inside the cabin," I suggested. "I'll run and grab it."

"All right, but hurry!" Jesco called as I

dashed back to the front door.

The door was unlocked and slightly ajar. Geez, that was stupid of us, not locking up, I thought. Anyone could've waltzed right in.

Then I realized what a silly thought that had been. Who was going to break into this cabin in the middle of nowhere?

I flicked on the light switch by the door. And nothing happened. The power was out.

That's strange, I thought. There must be some kind of fuse box in the cellar that my mom tore up.

I made my way through the dark room. The flashlight was in a drawer in the kitchen area.

Suddenly, I heard a floorboard creak. Not where I was walking. Somewhere off in the dark.

I stopped dead in my tracks and listened. Nothing. Nothing except the thumping of my heart.

I kept going and began poking around in the drawer. As fast as I could. Suddenly, I wanted to get out of that cabin. I just had a bad feeling. Where was that flashlight?

Finally, I yanked the entire drawer out and found it, all the way in the back.

All right, I thought. Now I can split . . .

I heard a door slam and a lock click shut.
The front door. The front lock.
Then I heard the growling.
Then I turned around . . . and screamed!

Chapter Thirty-Four

The figure snarling at me from across the room still stood on two legs, not four. But that was the only similarity between that figure and my mom.

Her entire body was covered with thick brown fur. I recognized a few bits of her outfit. But most of her clothes had been shredded to pieces. Her fingers and toes were almost gone. Her hands and feet were becoming paws!

Most shocking of all was my mom's face. Or what *used to be* her face.

Her mouth had stretched into a long, wolfish set of jaws. Her teeth had become fangs. Her nose had turned into a black, wet-looking snout. Her hair blended in with the hair that covered her face, her neck, her back.

The creature — my mom, a wolf-mom! — howled. And took another step toward me.

"Mom!" I cried. "Can't you understand me?

It's me, Iggy!"

I recognized the blue eyes staring back at me. They were my mom's eyes. I gazed into them, pleading. And I could tell she didn't recognize me.

"Mom, please!" I cried again.

She — *it!* — snarled in reply. And took another step toward me.

I took a step backward and bumped into the kitchen counter. I reached back to steady myself and felt the flashlight!

The wolf-mom growled and stretched her paw-hands in my direction. I reached into my pocket and pulled out the vial of hair and water.

This is my last chance, I thought grimly. It's now or never.

Then, out loud, I shouted, "Come on and get me!"

The wolf-mom snarled once again. And pounced!

I whipped the flashlight from behind my back and clicked it on. A beam of light hit her dead in the face. I jumped aside and she crashed into the kitchen counter.

The wolf-mom was blinded, flailing her arms wildly. I popped the cap off the vial with my thumb.

And jumped!

I hugged the wolf-mom around her furry neck. And with one quick motion, I poured the potion down her throat. Then I pushed myself off her body and fell to the floor.

The wolf-mom towered above me. She blinked. She could see again.

She could see me. And she looked madder than ever.

I closed my eyes and braced myself, waiting for the end.

Chapter Thirty-Five

My eyes were shut tight. Every muscle in my body was tense. I waited to be torn to shreds. To be devoured alive.

And nothing happened.

Slowly, I opened my eyes. There, sitting cross-legged on the floor in front of me was . . . my mother. Totally back to normal!

She rubbed her eyes with a torn shirt-sleeve. "Uhh," she moaned. "What happened? Where am I?"

"Mom!" I cried, dashing over and giving her a big hug. "Don't you remember? You were just about to kill me!"

My mom smiled at me and blinked. She looked sort of confused. "What are you talking about, sweetheart?" she asked. "I'd never hurt you!"

The door to the cabin burst open. Mole and Jesco rushed inside. With a dog. It was good old Kaiser Wilhelm!

"Oh, wow!" I cried. "Where'd you find him?"

"Out back," Jesco replied. "He came sniffing out of the woods while we were waiting for you. Then we heard all the screaming and thought the worst."

"But Mrs. Rockwell," Mole shouted, "you're back to normal. The potion worked!"

My mom put her hands on her hips and looked annoyed.

"All right," she said, turning to me. "I'm getting tired of everybody looking at me funny. I want a few answers. First of all, why are we standing here in the dark? Second, why are my clothes all ripped up? And third, who is this guy standing next to John, and why did they break the door down?"

I laughed, mostly out of relief.

"That's Jesco, Mom. He helped *us* help *you*. See, we crashed the van and then — Well, before we did that, we locked you in the cellar. And then we had to find the wolf that bit you. So we had this blow gun and . . . "

I stopped and took a deep breath. "Well, actually, it's a pretty long story. Maybe we should sit down."

"Maybe we'd better," my mom agreed.

Then she put her arm around my shoulder and gently kissed me on the forehead. Usually, if she did something like that in front of my friends, I'd be really embarrassed. But tonight, I didn't care.

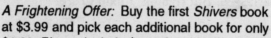